To Anton and Philippe.
I love you as borsch loves salt.

—Y. N.

Text and illustrations © 2022 Yevgenia Nayberg

Published in 2022 by Eerdmans Books for Young Readers
an imprint of Wm. B. Eerdmans Publishing Co., Grand Rapids, Michigan
www.eerdmans.com/youngreaders

Manufactured in the United States of America

30 29 28 27 26 25 24 23 22   1 2 3 4 5 6 7 8 9

ISBN 978-0-8028-5580-0

A catalog record of this book is available from the Library of Congress

Illustrations created with acrylic, pencils, and digital collage

I Hate BORSCH!

Written and illustrated by
Yevgenia Nayberg

EERDMANS BOOKS FOR YOUNG READERS

GRAND RAPIDS, MICHIGAN

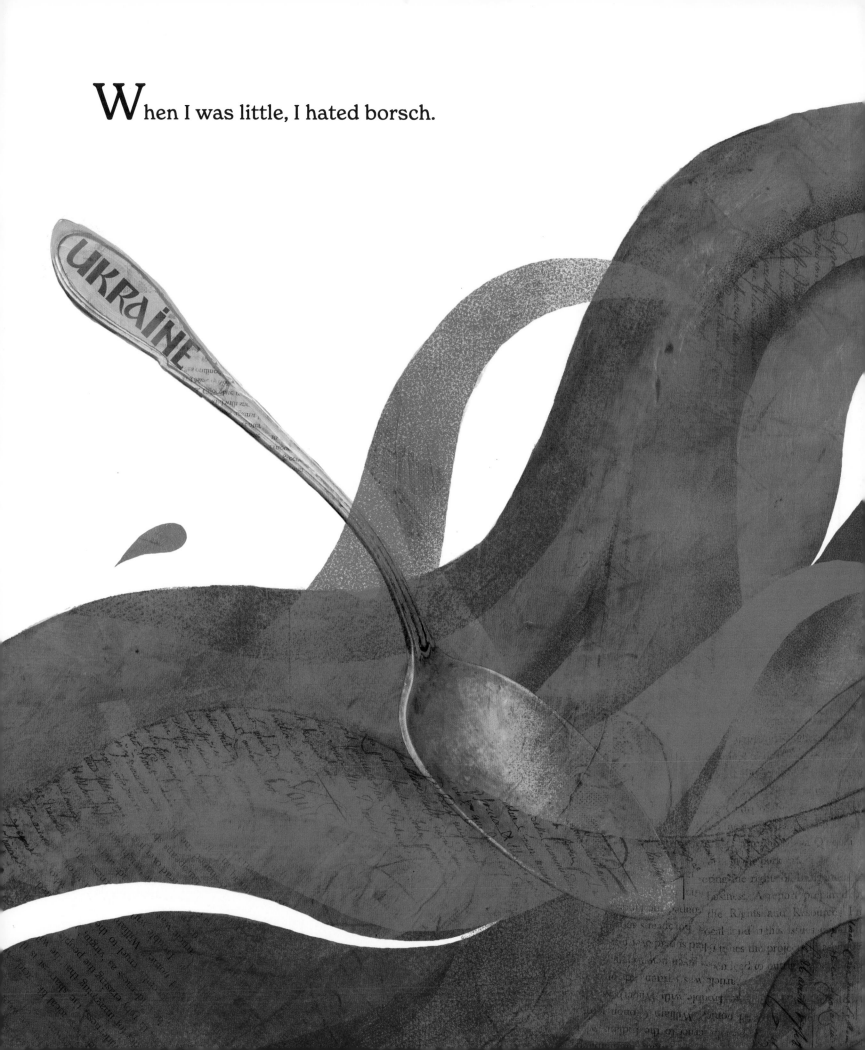

When I was little, I hated borsch.

I hated everything about it!

JUST ONE MORE SPOON . . .

The beets . . .

The cabbage . . .

The carrots . . .

And, above all, the slippery, slimy tomato!

In Ukraine, you were supposed to love
borsch from the first moment you picked up
the vegetables . . .

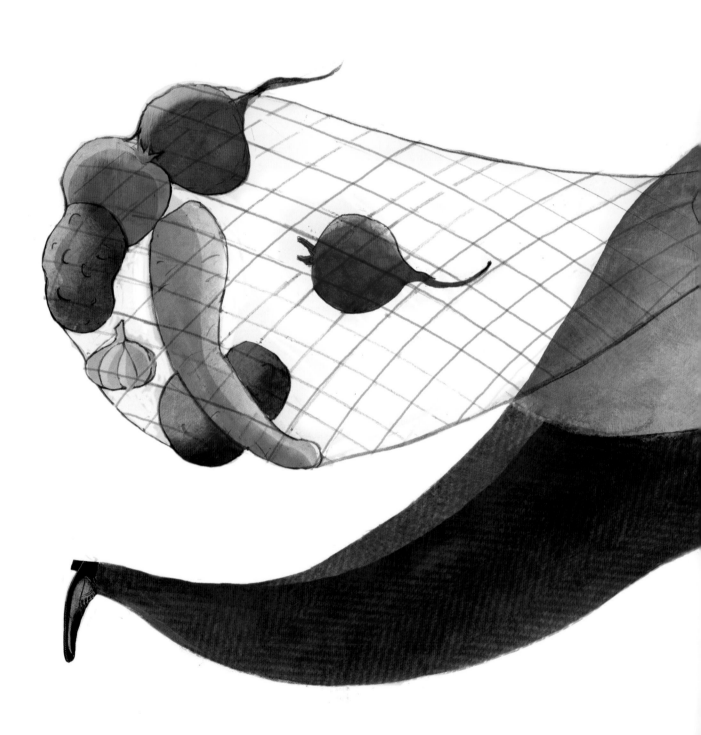

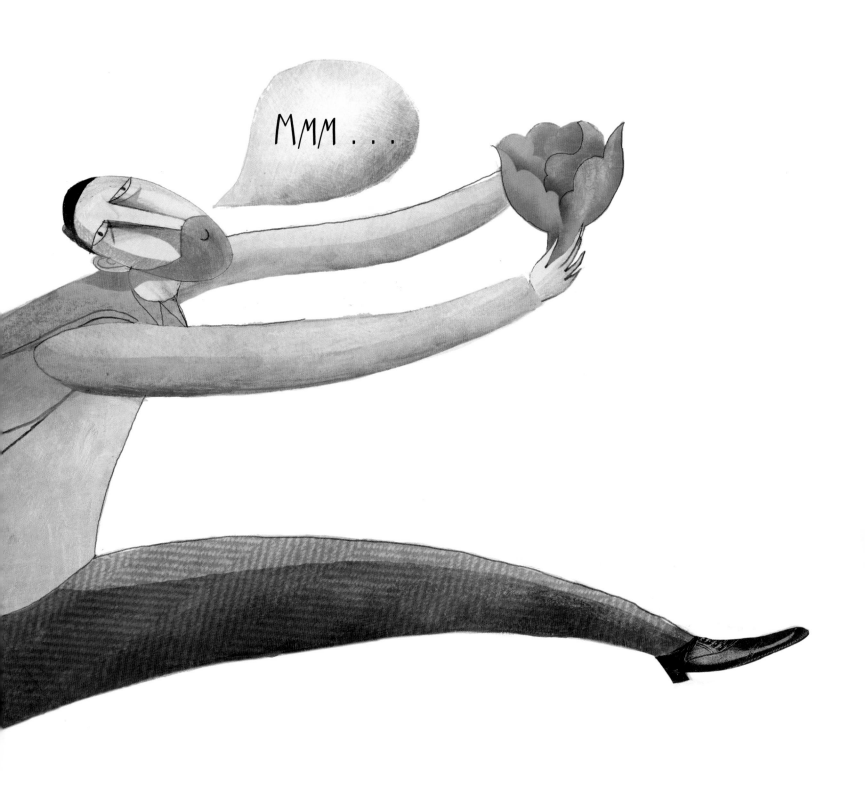

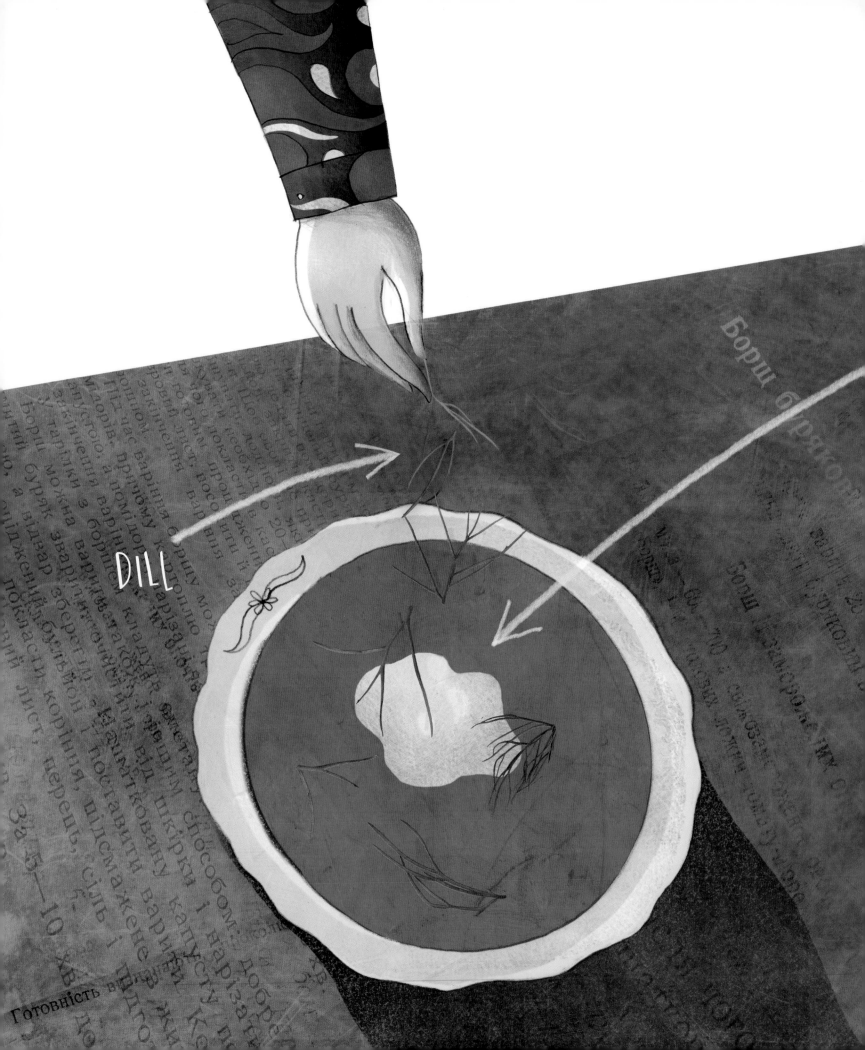

. . . to the final moment when it arrived at the table, steaming in a bowl.

I imagined myself as Robinson Crusoe,
stuck on a deserted island of sour cream
in a red sea of borsch.
All alone, surrounded by floating dill.

YOU WILL NOT LEAVE THE TABLE UNTIL
ALL THE BORSCH IS GONE!

If you did not like borsch, your life was hard.
Everything that grew in Ukraine went directly into
the pot:

The beets . . .

The cabbage . . .

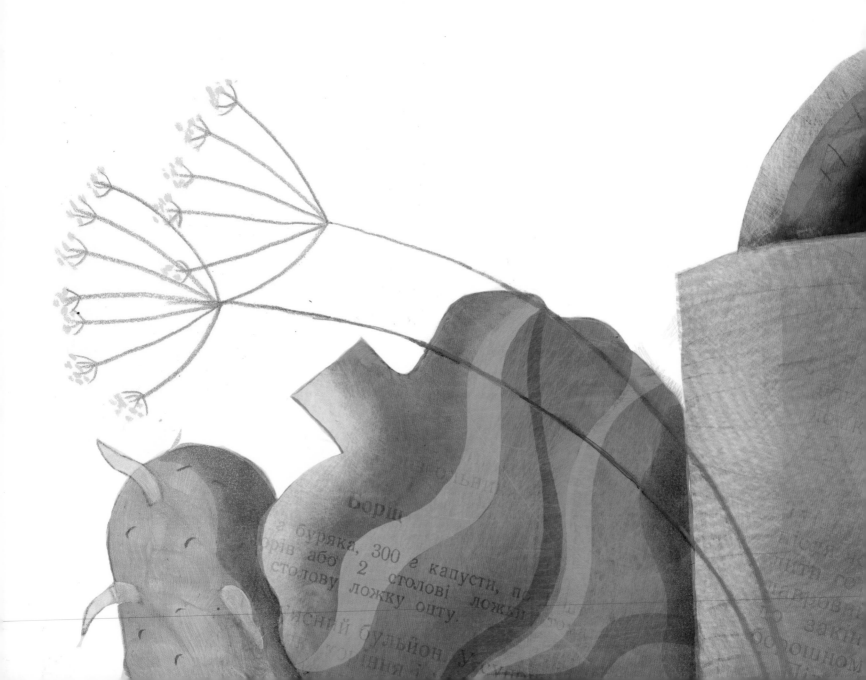

The carrots . . .

There wasn't much else to eat!

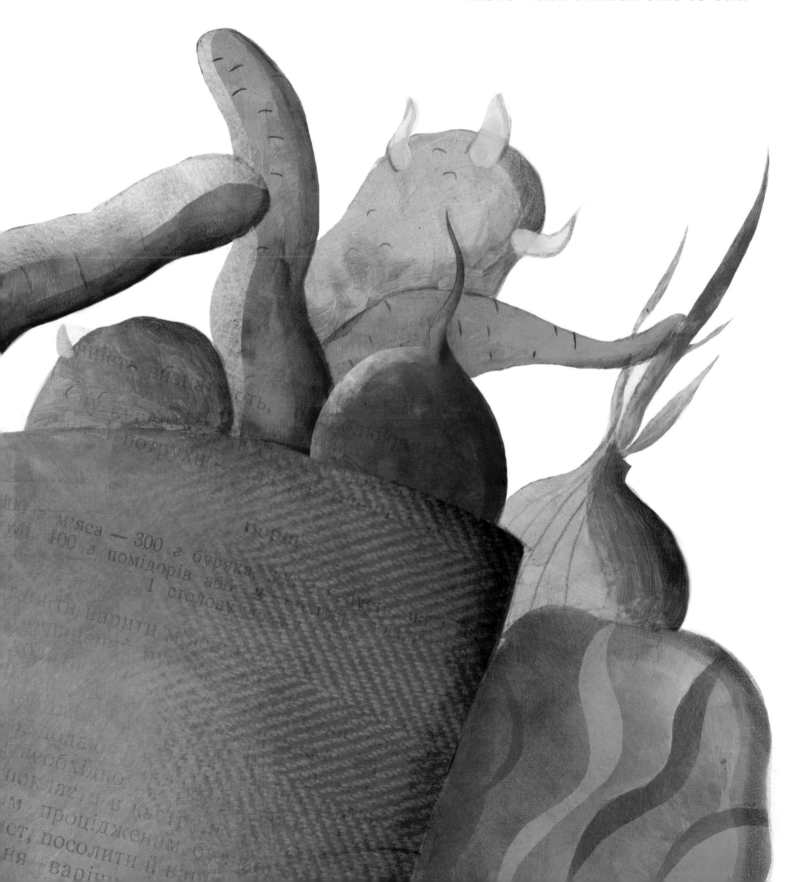

What about sunflowers? They grew everywhere!

Legend had it that brave Ukrainians defended their
castles by pouring borsch on enemies' heads.

I dreamed about doing just that!

Every grandma in Kiev owned the only true borsch recipe. Naturally, it was a secret recipe passed down by the czar's chef on his deathbed.

When we left for America, each grandma I knew gave me her recipe as a goodbye present.

YOUR HUSBAND WILL THANK YOU!

WHAT HUSBAND?

I pushed the recipes to the bottom of my suitcase.

In America, I learned new things about borsch.

They called it BORSCH T !

It came out of a jar and tasted like . . . nothing!

Another reason to never have borsch ever again!

From then on, I decided to eat only American foods:

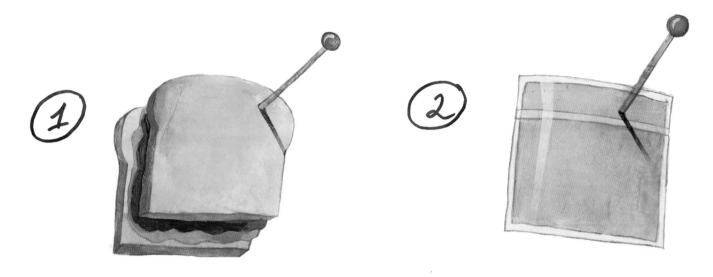

1 THE PEANUT BUTTER AND JELLY SANDWICH.

2 THE FLAT AND SHINY SQUARE CHEESE.

3 THE MYSTERIOUS PUMPKIN SPICE LATTE!

I ate through tons of American foods,

but there was something missing.

Maybe it was the red beets, dark and stormy against the white bowl.

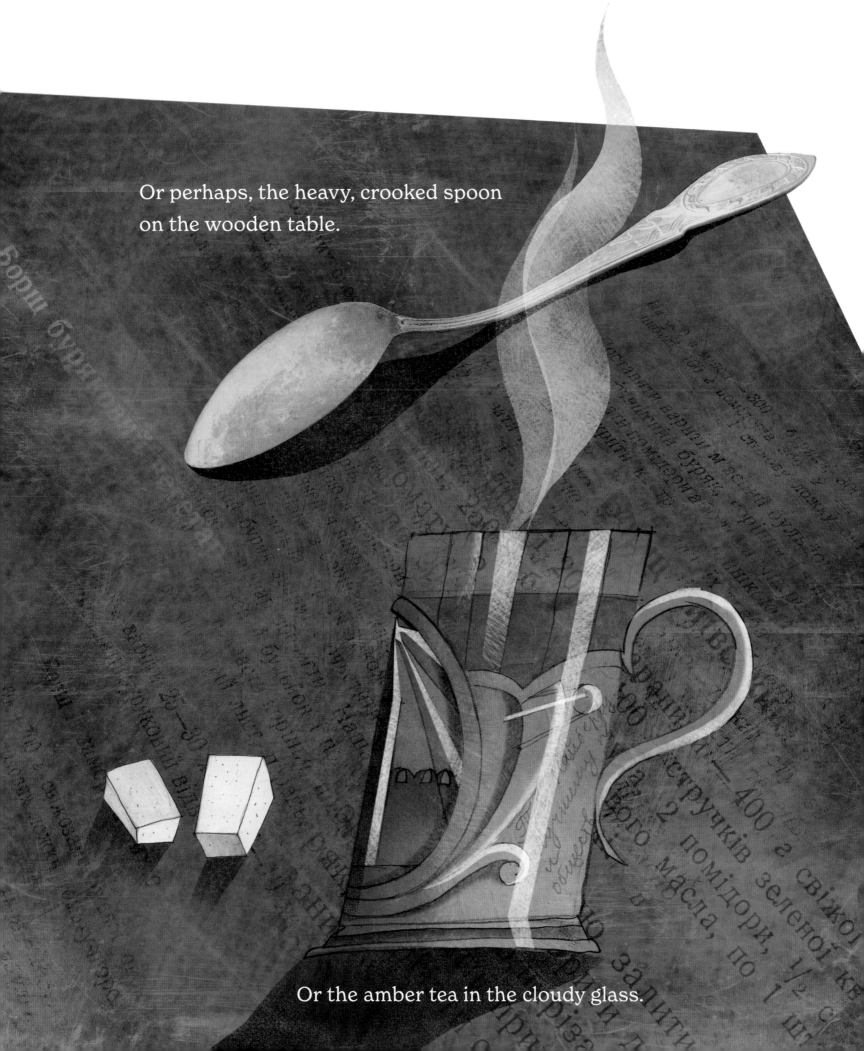

Or perhaps, the heavy, crooked spoon
on the wooden table.

Or the amber tea in the cloudy glass.

Today I opened my old suitcase.

There, underneath my tiny sweaters,
I found borsch recipes!
I laid them out on the floor.
I read them one by one.

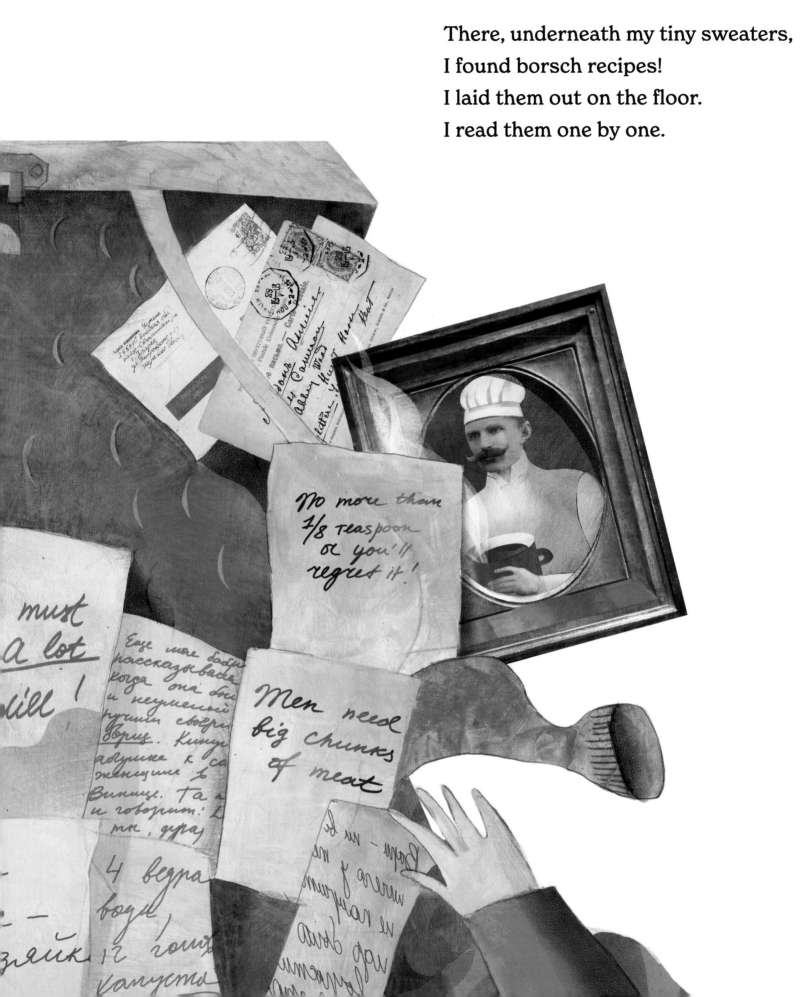

No more than 1/8 teaspoon or you'll regret it!

must
a lot
ill!

Men need big chunks of meat

And suddenly, I am transported back home.
I am sailing a borsch river on a carrot boat.
The sun is setting like a large beet.
Dill is blooming everywhere.

I arrange the vegetables on my kitchen counter:

The beets . . .
The cabbage . . .
The carrots . . .
The slippery, slimy
tomato . . .
And the bushy green dill!

Author's Note

There are as many borsch recipes as there are Ukrainian grandmas. And don't even get me started on the neighboring countries of Eastern Europe and their borsch recipes!

There is hot borsch and cold borsch, one with beans and another one with beef. There's a version with prunes, and one with mushrooms. There's even green borsch, which I refuse to discuss here.

It takes courage to share a borsch recipe. What would the grandmas think? And yet, I am going to do it.

This version of mine is vegan, at least until you add sour cream to your bowl at the end. (It is vegan by its nature, not because I removed some delicious ingredients.)

Here's What You Do:

Get the tiniest head of **green cabbage** you can find. Slice it in half and save another half for the time you decide to make some sauerkraut.

Roast and grate 4 small **beets**. (You can cheat and buy the scary-looking vacuum pack of ready-to-eat beets if you want.)

Peel and quarter 3 medium **potatoes**. Peel and grate 3 medium **carrots**.

Heat some neutral **oil**, like grapeseed or canola, in a large pot and drop the potatoes in. Let them get a bit of a tan, and drop in the carrots. Stir from time to time to make sure they don't burn.

Once they soften and brown a bit, fill the pot with boiling **water**, add a generous dash of **salt**, and a whole peeled **onion**. Important: now is the time to add a pinch of **sour salt**. Sour salt is another name for citric acid. You can find it at most supermarkets. Skip this step and end up with sad, brown borsch.

Next, add a heaping tablespoon of **tomato paste**. Drop in the grated beets, bring the borsch to a boil, then cover the pot and let it simmer for at least 30 minutes. I like to simmer for an hour.

While this is happening, slice the cabbage as thinly as humanly possible. Bring the borsch back to a boil and drop the cabbage in. Stir and turn the heat off immediately. This way the cabbage will retain some bite to it. Don't let it turn into a mushy mess!

Fish out and discard the onion. Taste and add more salt if needed. Crush a clove of **garlic** into the pot.

Ladle borsch into a bowl, add some **sour cream**, and sprinkle with fresh **dill**.

Any borsch will taste better the next day.

If this does not sound like the borsch your grandma makes, I apologize. I am sure she is a wonderful lady and a great cook.

Nevertheless, I stand by my borsch—as an artist, an omnivore, and a dual citizen.